The Tantrum

The Tantrum

by Kathryn Lasky

illustrated by Bobette McCarthy

MACMILLAN PUBLISHING COMPANY
NEW YORK

MAXWELL MACMILLAN CANADA
TORONTO

MAXWELL MACMILLAN INTERNATIONAL
NEW YORK   OXFORD   SINGAPORE   SYDNEY

Macmillan Publishing Company is part of the
Maxwell Communication Group of Companies.
Macmillan Publishing Company
866 Third Avenue, New York, NY 10022
Maxwell Macmillan Canada, Inc.
1200 Eglinton Avenue East, Suite 200
Don Mills, Ontario M3C 3N1
First edition
Printed in the United States of America

10   9   8   7   6   5   4   3   2   1
The text of this book is set in 17 point ITC Leawood Book.
The illustrations are rendered in watercolor.

Library of Congress Cataloging-in-Publication Data
Lasky, Kathryn.
The tantrum / by Kathryn Lasky ; illustrated by Bobette McCarthy.
p.   cm.
Summary: A little girl has a tantrum and disrupts her whole household.
ISBN 0-02-751661-X
[1. Temper tantrums—Fiction.]   I. McCarthy, Bobette, ill.
II. Title.
PZ7.L3274Tan   1993   [E]—dc20   92-3701

For Bobby and Mikie, with love
—B.M.

I had a tantrum today.

I slammed my head against the bed and kicked my feet so hard they left scuff marks on the wall.

I roared until my face was purple and spit my brother
out the door when he said "Shut up."

And when my mom said "Be calm," I tore up a drawing
I was making and told her it had been for her.

And she said, "Let's ignore this behavior!"

So I flung all the little pieces down the stairs, and
when she said, "Pick them up, Grace," I beat my fists
on the carpet and cried "no fair" until my head hurt.

And then my dad said "Control yourself."

That made me even madder.

So I slammed a door or two.

And then my brother said the worst thing of all.

"Gracie's having a little tantrum, a fit, a fitsky."

I felt my face turn monster green and tight as
a wet knot in a shoelace.

Boy, was I mad. He was trying to shrink my fit,
my tantrum, into something little and silly.

Something kind of furry and fluffy and cute.

It wasn't any such thing!

My fit was big and full of roars. My cheeks were hot
and slick. My head ached from all the thunder inside it.
And remember, there are scuff marks on the wall.

Remember that, because when I went upstairs again and saw the marks I couldn't remember what my fit was about. Do you?

I wanted my mom to buy me gum, was that it?

Or was it something about sharing?

I don't always like to share.

My brother once had a tantrum, you know,
about sharing, when he was little.
He threw himself down on the sidewalk.
My mother thought he would crack his head.
He didn't.

But she had to pick him up and carry him inside
so he wouldn't really hurt himself.

She had to try and make him safe during his tantrum.

My mother says she wishes sometimes she could have tantrums. But she can't. She's grown-up. That would look silly—grown-ups banging their heads and kicking walls. So my mom gets to be the boss instead, to scold us and make us safe when we have fits and tantrums.

And boy, does she get tired,

especially when I have mine.

I'll grow up too, someday, and not have any more fits or tantrums, because scuff marks from big shoes look real silly on a wall.

DATE DUE

JUL 2 5 2007		
DEC 1 0 2007		
NOV 2 2 2013		
OCT 3 0 2021		

CATALOGED 4   NC

GAYLORD M2